Professor Cane

By Aurelia Yates

Copyright © 2023 by Aurelia Yates

All rights reserved.

Visit my website at
https://www.AureliaYatesAuthor.com

Cover Designer: Christy Pierce Photography, LLC
Professional Photographer - Christy Pierce Photography LLC

Editor: https://personaltouchediting.godaddysites.com/

Models: Lauren Estes-Bailey

https://linktr.ee/laurenestesfit

No part of this book may be reproduced or transmitted in any form or by any means, electronic or mechanical, including photocopying, recording, or by any information storage and retrieval system without the written permission of the author, except for the use of brief quotations in a book review. This book is a work of fiction. Names, characters, places, and incidents either are products of the author's imagination or are used fictitiously. Any resemblance to actual persons, living or dead, events, or locales is entirely coincidental.

ISBN: 979-8-9867542-7-7

TABLE OF CONTENTS

TITLE
1

Copyrights
2

Follow Aurelia
5

Warning
6

Chapter One
7

Chapter Two
12

Chapter Three
17

Chapter Four
22

Chapter Five
27

Chapter Six
31

Chapter Seven
35

Chapter Eight
39

Chapter Nine
44

Chapter Ten
49

Chapter Eleven
55

Chapter Twelve
59

Chapter Thirteen
63

About The Author
68

FOLLOW AURELIA ON

https://www.goodreads.com/author/show/22689072.Aurelia_Yates

https://www.bookbub.com/profile/aurelia-yates

https://www.facebook.com/aureliayatesauthor

https://www.instagram.com/aureliayatesauthor/

https://www.tiktok.com/@aureliayatesauthor

WARNING

This book is rated R; not appropriate for readers under 18 years of age; contains elements of sex, cheating, and language.

CHAPTER ONE

Jackson

Stopping at the front desk, I scan my membership card.

The hostess greets me with a mischievous glint in her eyes.

"Good evening, Mr. Largewood." She licks her lips, and her eyes linger on my body, slowly coming to blatantly rest on my crotch.

"Good evening Tonya," I smirk.

Her eyes flicker up. "Let me know if you need,"—glancing back down at my uninterested cock, she purrs—"assistance with anything."

I nod and continue to make my way to my regular booth in the club.

Tonya was one of my students, and I have no interest in her. I don't even bother to ask why she's working here because she graduated last year and should have a successful career in marketing. She was a bright student, but it seems she would prefer using her body rather than her mind.

Viper is owned by a close friend of mine, Mitchell Gray. We were college roommates and have stayed in touch with our other two roommates, Harrison and Shane.

Mitchell spared no expense to make his club the best strip joint in the state of Pennsylvania. The outside of the club looks like an old, dilapidated building, while the inside is fitted with the finest furnishings, paintings, and materials.

Only members are allowed in to enjoy the women and drinks. Everyone undergoes an extensive background and financial check. Once you're in, you have access to the most beautiful, young, and skilled women as they flaunt their bodies for your viewing pleasure.

Most of them are working here to pay their way through college, and I see them on campus, but I also do my best not to be seen. That's why I take my usual corner booth.

We sat in the same booth when I met Mitchell at the club for a drink. It's a dark corner booth, and the lights cast a shadow over your face so no one can make out who you are. I had no interest in coming for a hookup. Pussy is easy for me to get, but when I saw Candy, I knew I had to make her mine.

I can't get the image out of my head of how she would look with her legs spread wide for me. Her pussy glistening with her arousal, and hearing her begging for me to shove my cock into her sweet, wet pussy.

Fuck! My cock is already getting hard, straining against my zipper. I give it a tight squeeze to ease some of the pressure.

The first sight of her had me hooked. I came here every week since, wanting to get another glance at her. She already has me by the balls and leads me around by the head of my cock. I can only imagine how much of a goner I'll be when I finally get a taste.

I only have one problem. She is the only woman who shows no interest in me, and it drives me to the point of insanity. I make it a point to appear at the doorway to art class every morning, and she walks by me without glancing my way. The other young women in her class stop and flirt, but not Ms. Cane.

I know she's almost done with school. She doesn't have much left. It pisses me off that she has to work here to pay her way through college.

Not for much longer.

I've been trying to devise a plan to get her into my bed, and with her graduation coming up, I finally have the solution I need.

I sit in the booth. The lights are dim, and I know she won't be able to see me from here. I wouldn't dare make an advancement toward her here. Just watching her from a distance gives me something to look forward to each evening.

I know she's working tonight. Mitchell mentioned she's working Fridays through Tuesdays in order to get some extra money. Something about going on a bachelorette trip.

I've been sitting in my booth for twenty minutes when Candy makes her appearance on the stage.

The men sitting at the bar front and center for her performance start making catcalls, and my jaw clenches. I want to rip their tongues out, but I remind myself she is doing this for the money.

She doesn't go home with anyone, and that pleases me. I know because I watch her every night from inside my car. I want to ensure she gets to her car without anyone bothering her.

As she moves about the stage and swings her leg above her head, I have to restrain myself from jumping up and grabbing her from the stage.

The thin material barely covers that sweet pussy, not that I've had the privilege if tasting it… at least not yet. Pasties cover her nipples, and I have the primal urge to pull them off with my teeth. I would prefer it in private, but I'm not opposed to doing it publicly.

She moves to work the pole, and as always, she looks oblivious to her surroundings. Her eyes look beyond the men. I thought she was looking at me a few times, but I was wrong. She's lost somewhere in her mind.

The way she moves is perfection, as if she's painting a canvas around the metal pole. Each movement she makes is a beautiful brush stroke.

Candy is her stage name, but I know her given name is Catherine. Catherine Cane is simply captivating. She steals each breath I take, holding them hostage. I would gladly give them up to be lost in her for one night of heated sex.

Every time I see her, my desire to have her becomes stronger. If I approach her here, she'll never see me as someone to be with. I've seen the way she brushes men off, and I can't say I blame her. The men here are too fucking pathetic. I'm not one of them. I'm successful, good looking, educated, and have a thick cock that could pleasure her body in so many ways. My tongue alone could bring her more pleasure than any of the pitiful fucks in this club. My only problem is getting her in my bed, but I'm a resourceful man. I always get what I want, even if it's playing dirty.

Catherine Cane, you will be mine.

CHAPTER TWO
Catherine

I wrap my leg around the steel pole and swing myself around it, blocking out the loud music and the eager men who sit around the stage.

They hold their money with one hand and their dicks with other. I'm happy to take their money. Their dicks ... they can keep.

I have no interest in becoming anything like my co-worker, Sandy. I can tell she was a beautiful woman at one time. Her soft features are hard now, her skin looks like leather from spending too much time in a tanning bed, and her eyes always have dark circles under them.

Sandy likes to party. She's always taking home some drunk slob who offers a little money so she can get high or have a place to crash. It's sad, but no matter how much one of the other girls offers to help her, she refuses.

I'm here to accomplish my goal—pay off my

student loans—not to do drugs or hook up with the sad men who come in to cheat on their wives. Viper offers me great pay, and I get to make my own hours. I need the flexibility for my classes.

My graduation is coming, and I will finally have my master's degree to become an art teacher. I want to be able to teach at the college level, and after all the late nights of working, studying and barely sleeping, it's finally paying off.

I've applied for several positions but haven't heard back from them. I still have high hopes of hearing something. It's just a waiting game.

Twirling, I stretch my leg out and whirl it around to lock my ankle around the metal bar. I look off into the distance and see the same shadowy figure that's there every night.

It's a man's silhouette. I can tell by their large, squared shoulders. He comes every night, but he doesn't make himself known. He just sits and observes. Maybe he's just the type of person who would rather watch. Everyone has their own kink or fantasy.

There's just something about him that my eyes are drawn to. I do my best to look dazed, as though I'm not searching for a hint of a glimpse of his face, but I'm not sure if he can tell.

I won't act on my need to know who he is. I refuse to date a man who comes to a joint like this every night, even if it's a high society strip club.

When I meet someone, I want them to only have eyes for me because they care about what's inside, not how they can take pleasure from the outside.

My college, Buckton University, is a two-hour drive

from work. I chose this club because I knew no one from my school would be coming here. It's too far from school and too far from my family, who live in the opposite direction of my college.

I'm not ashamed of what I do. Well, maybe a little bit, but college is expensive, and I don't want to be drowning in debt when I finally graduate.

When I do a sit spin on the pole, a man seated on a bar stool reaches up and grabs my ankle. I try to kick him off, but he pulls harder, making me fall on the platform.

"Mother fucker!"

"Come here, baby," he slurs. "Why don't you suck on my dick, and I'll give you a night you'll never forget."

Fucking gross! Men like this piss me off.

"I would if you had enough to stick in my mouth," I spit out.

His face turns red, and his friends laugh. He tries to launch at me, but security gets to him in time to pull him back and show his ass to the door.

Fucking prick!

When I stand up, I see the shadow of the man from earlier standing by his booth. I squint, trying harder to see if I can make out any details, but as usual, I'm unable to.

I dust myself off and walk off stage. I've had enough for the night, and I'm ready to head home.

Getting to my dressing area, I pull off my wig. Tonight, I was a redhead with straight hair that came down to my mid-back. I pop out the green contacts and put them away. My normal blue eyes shine bright, looking back at me in the mirror.

I only wear the wig and contacts when I work. I haven't seen anyone I know, but if I did, I really don't want to have to explain myself.

After I change clothes and remove all my makeup, I gather my bag and walk out the back door.

Usually, I ask one of the guys to walk me out, but I didn't want to have to wait on them tonight.

When I step outside, chills run up my arms and down my spine, causing me to tremble as my breath begins to quicken. Somewhere in the dark, there's a set of eyes on me, and I can feel their gaze sweeping over me from head to toe. I survey the parking lot, trying to look for anyone, but again, I see nothing.

I do my best to walk normally and not show that the hairs on the back of my neck are standing up on high alert.

I hear sounds of laughter and stop. Turning slowly, I see a couple in the back alley making out, and I exhale. He pushes her to her knees and grabs his cock, placing it in her mouth. The sounds of her wet slurps and gagging echo off the two brick buildings they're between.

Turning back around, I pick up speed with each step I take toward my car with my heart in my throat. The feeling of being watched never leaves me. When I'm two steps away, I unlock it with my keyless remote and jump into the driver's seat. Slamming it shut, I press the lock button.

Fuck! Why do I feel so uneasy every night I work?

I crank the car and get ready to make the two-hour journey back to my apartment, which I share with three other girls. Joey, one of my roommates, I've been friends with since our freshman year at BU. We're both getting our master's in education. Claire and Susie are in their senior year and majoring in education, too. We've all had classes together and get along well.

But first, I need something to settle my nerves.

Pulling into a fast-food place, I grab a coffee and turn up the radio to make my long journey back home.

CHAPTER THREE
Catherine

I've received letters back from every position I applied for. All were rejection letters because I have no experience. How am I supposed to get experience when no one will give it to me? Ugh.

Blowing out air, I feel helpless and defeated at not being able to have something by now lined up for after graduation.

I only have a month left in this semester, then I'll have my degree, but it seems even with that important document, I won't be able to snag a job.

No experience. Pfft.

Slamming my suitcase closed, I blow out a deep breath. I'll have to pick up extra shifts at Viper, and the thought makes my stomach drop. I had planned on working just weekends after I got a job in my field. I want to pay off my student loans as quickly as possible, so I guess there's no other choice.

Rolling my suitcase out of my bedroom, I put the

job search behind me. My face must show my worry lines because Joey comes over and gives me a reassuring hug.

"Don't worry Cat. Something is going to happen. You're going to get an amazing job!"

Joey always seems to know exactly how I'm feeling.

"I know. I just wish it would come before this semester ends." I sigh.

"It will. Now, let's go. The beach is calling my name, and the hotel has cabana boys to wait on us hand and foot," she squeals.

We're headed to the beach during our fall break for Joey's bachelorette party. She's getting married on New Year's Day at her parent's ranch in upstate Pennsylvania.

After five hours and twenty minutes of being cramped in a Mini Cooper, we park at the elaborate condo Joey's parents rented for us.

Peeling myself out of the backseat, I stretch out my legs with a groan. I'm average height, standing at five-six, but still too tall for the backseat of a Mini Cooper.

"Cat, can you go to the office and get our keys, please?" Joey begs.

"Yeah, do we need a cart?" I ask.

Joey looks into Claire's car and just shakes her head. I laugh because we were both cramped in the back seat, completely miserable. There's no room for extra luggage. We each packed one bag, so there's really no need for a large cart.

I head toward the door that says office. When I start to open it, the door flies open, and I gasp. Mr. Largewood is standing in the doorway without a shirt. The sun shines off his wet olive skin, making the muscles more defined in his broad shoulders.

Have I died and gone to Heaven?

My eyes trail down to the swim trunks hanging low on his hips and that dark, happy trail that leads into them looks like a welcome mat.

My mouth goes dry.

When my eyes trail back up his body, I try to remember every freckle, every scar, and every hair on his perfect physique.

His brown eyes shine with mischievous intent.

My clit starts to throb, and arousal soaks my panties. I clench my thighs together to alleviate some of the ache, hoping he won't notice. My nipples are hardened peaks that could cut glass hidden behind my sports bra.

"Ms. Cane. Are you following me?" his deep voice booms.

The corners of his perfectly full lips curl up, and I can't speak.

I nod.

He laughs. "You are following me?"

I shake my head furiously. "No… no… I meant…" I wet my lips to speak, and I notice how his eyes follow my tongue. "I meant to say no. Sorry. I'm here for my friend's bachelorette party."

He smiles, showing me his perfectly straight white teeth, and steps forward, making me push my back against the door so he can get by.

He surprises me when he stops directly in front of me and turns to face me. Putting his hand on the wall over my head, he leans down to my ear.

"Too bad, but if you change your mind, I'm in fifty-four. I'm going to grab a shower. Should I wait for you?"

His lips brush against my neck, and I whimper from the throbbing of my pussy.

How the fuck could this be happening to me?

I see him every day, but I'm too shy to speak. I laugh internally. I'm a freaking stripper showing my tits for money, but the one man I would be happy to give a private lap dance to, I get my tongue tied up into a knot.

Fucking great!

I clear my throat and turn to him. "Mr. Largewood."

He smiles. "Ms. Cane, do I make you nervous?"

Goosebumps erupt across my skin when his spearmint breath hits my nose, assaulting my senses. His lips are so close, it wouldn't take but a slight tilt toward him for our lips to touch.

Someone clears their throat, and Joey stands outside the office door. Mr. Largewood pushes back, not taking his eyes off me.

"Ms. Vann, I was just telling Ms. Cane I'm in fifty-four," His eyes trail down my body. "If you need anything, just let me know."

He steps back and looks at Joey, giving her a nod, then he walks away.

The air releases from my lungs, and I feel my chest collapse in on itself, launching me forward.

Joey and I look at each other with wide eyes. With the biggest grin on her face, she locks our arms together, walking into the office.

"Fuck, Cat. He's so fucking hot! I wonder how large his wood is!" She says the last part with curiosity.

She's not the only one who wants to know.

We get checked in, and when the lady behind the counter tells us we're in room fifty-three, my knees go weak.

How am I going to be able to sleep with Mr. Largewood sleeping or, worse, fucking someone next door?

We thank her and go back outside to grab our bags and get on the elevator to the fifth floor. When we get to our door and are about to unlock it, the door to fifty-four opens, and a man with a tan and blond curls comes out with a smile that would win over any woman.

Claire drops her jaw but quickly recovers. "Hi," she says as she places her finger to her lips, sucking at the tip. Her eyes never leave his lips.

I roll my eyes at her flirting skills. How could she be so good at it? I envy that outgoing personality and the way she's so comfortable around men.

I know what I do to make money, but I transform into someone else when I'm on that stage. I'm not Catherine. I'm Candy. Candy is the side of me I can let loose and enjoy being comfortable in my own skin without being criticized for the imperfections of my body.

CHAPTER FOUR

Jackson

As I walk back to the pool, I can't think of anything else but wanting to pin Catherine up against that office door and nail her to it with my hard cock.

When I reach my lounge chair, I grab my towel and throw it to the side. Harrison comes out of the elevator, looking smug. When he sits down, he throws his feet up and tilts his head back.

I can tell he's searching for something or maybe someone. The horny bastard!

"Well?" Harrison asks.

I look over at the golden boy and shake my head. I had to talk Harrison into coming with me for the weekend. He abruptly refused to come when he found out where we would be staying. Harrison can be a snob.

I had to pull out the "You owe me" card.

"Take one for the team" is what he told me when he begged me to double date with him a few months back. All because he wanted to get into a certain blonde's panties.

Worst night of my life. I still remind him of it to this day, and he just laughs at my expense. *Fucker!*

I knew Catherine would be here. I found out through Mitchell. Thank goodness for him. He's tried to start up conversations with her about various things to keep me informed of her plans for after college.

I've had to roadblock her applications for applying to other positions. I'm not proud of the actions I've taken, but if they let me get my dick wet by sliding into that pretty little cunt of hers, it's what I have to do. Well, let's just say it will be well worth it.

I knew she would be checking in today, so we arrived yesterday. I've been going to the office non-stop to try to run into her. Thank God I finally did because I was running out of excuses to be there. I think the old lady at the desk thought I was senile, asking for toilet paper and towels and what time check-out was. I was starting to think I would lose it if I had to face her again.

"I ran into her coming out of the office," I say quietly.

Harrison turns his face toward me with white teeth shining. "Well, did you—"

"No." I stop the fucker before he has a chance to finish.

Harrison is too much like Mitchell. Their dicks lead them around. They don't have an ounce of discretion in them. When they want someone in their bed, they make a move to go in for the kill without building up to it. Putting work into getting pussy is not for them.

A woman gives it up, or they move on to the next one.

"Damn." He lets out a breath, "I was hoping you nailed her so we could get out of this shitty place." He looks back up at the condo building. "Lucky for you, I found someone to occupy my time while I'm here."

I roll my eyes and lay my head back. I try my best not to think of Catherine, but I fail when I hear her voice.

Tilting my head slightly, I see her and her friends coming out in their swimsuits and gathering up lounge chairs to group together.

Fuck me!

Catherine bends over on the opposite side of the pool with her round ass in front of my sight, and my dick twitches in my swim trunks.

Harrison sits a little straighter and I punch his arm. *Fucker better not be looking at her ass.*

"What the fuck was that for?" he whispers.

"Don't look at her ass," I growl.

"I wasn't. I was looking at her friend's," he smirks. "I'm going to give it to her so good."

"Mr. Largewood."

I jump. Fuck. I turn to the voice, and it's Joey Vann. She's only standing two feet away. I cringe. Shit, I hope she didn't hear us talking.

"Ms. Vann, are you enjoying yourself?"

She grins like a Cheshire cat, and I know we've been caught.

"So far. You know, we're going out to dinner tonight. Why don't you two join us?" She smiles.

Maybe she didn't hear us.

"We wouldn't want to impose," I glance over to see Catherine looking at us with her jaw slack. "Only if you promise everyone would be okay with us tagging along."

Joey's smile widens, and I can tell she's up to something.

"It won't be an imposition at all." She looks over at Catherine. "Hey, Cat, bring me your phone."

Catherine leans down to her bag, and her tits hang over.

I catch myself growing hard.

I have to close my eyes and start citing the presidents of the United States. My hands shake with the need to be filled with Catherine's perky tits.

When I hear her raspy voice, I open my eyes to the most glorious sight.

Catherine is standing next to me in a pink bikini that covers more than I've seen her wearing in the strip club, and somehow, she looks sexier. I look at that pussy I've imagined so many times with me eating it like it was my last meal. Her bikini bottom is flat against it, and I can only imagine her pussy is slick.

She hands her phone to Joey, and Joey hands it to me.

"Here, give us your number. We can text you the name and address of where we decide to go for dinner. Six o'clock, okay?"

Catherine looks at Joey, and I can tell she's a bit shaken. Does she not want me to go? I can't get a read on her.

Entering my number, I then hand the phone to Catherine. I feel a little spark when her hand touches mine, but she yanks it out of my grip, leaving me wondering if I shouldn't go.

25

I don't think about it too much because whether she wants me or not, I'm going to have her under me soon. I just need to be patient. My plan is set in motion, and I don't fail when I want something.

CHAPTER FIVE

Catherine

When Mr. Largewood hands me my phone back, I nearly get knocked off my feet when a sharp spark occurs just from a brush of his fingers.

I'm left speechless.

Joey pushes me by the arm, letting me know it's time to walk back to our chairs.

When we reach our chairs, I slide my sunglasses on, pick up my book, and flop on my back in the chair. Keeping my eyes on Mr. Largewood, I pretend to read.

God, he's breathtaking. His thick hair is cut short and faded. His broad shoulders beg me to hold them while I ride his cock.

Frustrated, I throw my book down and get up to go in the water.

I need to cool off.

Entering the pool, the water is lukewarm but still able to cool my raging hormones. I dip my head under the water and come back up, pushing my hair back. Swimming out to the edge, I feel something bite the back of my thigh, causing a scream to escape my lips.

I turn around in a panic when Mr. Largewood comes to the surface, looking like the best wet dream come to life.

He smiles and inches toward me, making my heart rate pick up. I press my back into the cement wall of the pool.

When he's close to me, our breaths begin to mingle as one. My legs part, and he fits in between them like they're welcoming him into me. When he pivots his hips, I feel how hard and how large of a man he truly is. A moan escapes my lips.

"You like that," he whispers in my ear. "Oh Catherine, you make me so hard."

My eyes flutter as he keeps pressing into me. I'm so lost in the moment, I'm almost seeing stars.

I reach up to place my hands on his shoulders and feel the muscles underneath my hands flex.

"Don't stop," I beg, my voice strained with lust.

He starts to grind against my pussy, and I'm almost there, just a little more, but then the fucker pulls back. My eyes pop open, and I see him swim backward with a sinful grin.

All of a sudden, I go from horny to fucking pissed.

I'm on the edge of the pool and on the edge of an orgasm, but now I'm left with needs and feelings destroyed. I can't believe I let him bring me to that point.

What is wrong with me? Get it together, Catherine.

I dive into the pool, trying my best to wash away the humiliation I'm left with. When I come up to the surface, I'm glad to see no one was watching my interaction with Largewood.

Getting out of the pool and striding over to my chair, I look at my friend with a huff.

"Joey,"—I start gathering up my stuff—"I'm going to go nap before dinner tonight."

"Okay, we'll see you in a bit."

Without sparing a glance toward Mr. Largewood, I dash off to the elevator. The doors are almost shut when a large hand grabs the edge of one of the doors and stops it from closing.

FUCK! It's him.

"Mr. Largewood—"

"Please, Jackson," he cuts me off. His deep voice booms, bouncing off the steel walls and straight to my pussy.

"Jackson," I clear my throat. "What the hell—"

His arm stretches out, and his hand runs into my hair quickly. All of a sudden, I'm up against him, and his lips are on mine while his other hand snakes down my back and pushes me into his cock. When his hand reaches my ass, he gives it a hard, punishing squeeze.

It feels too good. I can't help but want to sink into the kiss, but my brain finally wakes up.

I try to push against him, but he's too firm. I'm not even moving him in the slightest.

Breaking our kiss, I try to put some distance between us.

"What the hell was that about in the pool?" I look at him with outrage.

"I was just getting a small taste." He nips my bottom lip. "It seems like you enjoyed yourself," he says with a cocky grin.

I want to slap that grin right off his pretty face.

"This can't be happening." I want to wash away the shame of exposing myself to him in an intimate way, but I also want to indulge myself and drink him up like he's the finest glass of wine I've ever had.

His hands feel like soft feathers as they run down my arms. They tickle my skin, causing shivers to run up my spine.

"So much more could be happening," he says, eyes pinning me to the floor.

The doors open, and it feels like it's been a decade since we stepped into the elevator.

Not acknowledging what he says, I gather what strength I have left and pull myself to my condo. I swipe my key, but his arm comes up to stop me from entering.

"What are you looking for, Ms. Cane?" His breath fans across my neck. "Tell me, and I'll make it happen."

Pushing his arm down, I step inside then turn to face his beautiful body.

"Unless you can help me find a job, you're useless to me." I close the door, cutting him off when he opens his mouth.

I know Mr. Largewood isn't a bad guy. Lord knows I've watched him over the years. Hell, I and every other girl in college has been obsessed with his good looks and charming ways.

I'm just a little unsure of what to make of his intentions in the pool. Not to mention his cornering me in the office earlier today.

CHAPTER SIX

Jackson

Harrison and I are dressed and loaded in the car after I received Joey's text message about where to meet them.

After Catherine shut the door in my face, I plastered the biggest smile on my face. Tonight, I plan on putting my plan into action.

"You've been way too fucking happy ever since you disappeared this afternoon. Did you finally get to nail Catherine to the wall?"

I stay silent.

Harrison knows all about my obsession with Catherine. All my friends know how obsessed I have been with her.

There's no way I'll be bragging when I finally sink my cock into her. She's not the kind of girl who gives it up easily, and I know I will have to work for it. If that doesn't work like I know it won't, I'll have to go to Plan B.

We pull into the parking lot and park.

"Come on, fucker, let's go. I'm starving and glad this place doesn't look like a shit hole," Harrison barks out.

We climb out of the four-door sedan and walk into the seafood restaurant. The aroma from the kitchen hits my nose, making me want to sit and eat. When I turn to look through the open windows that line the wall, I spot what I have been wanting to eat all day long.

Catherine is sitting by a window while the breeze blows from the ocean through the windows and brushes her hair, making it float back from her face. She looks angelic with her long blonde locks blowing back.

I stand frozen until Harrison slaps my chest.

"Come on, pussy boy, let's go." He bounces on his feet and takes off in Catherine's direction, taking a seat by her friend.

Her friend is beautiful but nowhere near as beautiful as Catherine.

I pull out a seat next to Catherine, hoping she saved it for me, but I know better. When I sit down, her body stiffens, and she doesn't make eye contact. She turns her head, looking out in the dark toward the ocean.

Another breeze comes off the ocean and blows past me with a soft vanilla fragrance. I lean in Catherine's direction without being too obvious, instantly getting hard.

The soft fragrance comes in stronger waves, and I can't help the need and want I have from becoming stronger. My desire to wrap her around me and bury myself deep inside her as sweet heat overtakes us both to the ecstasy of a powerful orgasm.

I reach down and adjust my cock. It's hard and in an uncomfortable position.

"Have you been here before?" I ask Catherine.

Catherine winces, and her head shoots up, glaring at Joey across the table. When she bends down to rub her leg I notice for the first time how short her shorts are. I could easily slide my finger into the hemline to rub through her folds.

"I've been here a couple of times," Catherine says, pulling me out of my lustful thoughts.

"Is the food any good?" I'm doing my best to keep her engaged in a conversation.

Her body loosens, and the tension she had when I first took a seat dissolves.

"It's very good," she says as she looks at me.

It's the first time I notice how blue her eyes are. They're the perfect shade of the sky, the light blue that could make any bad day brighter. Her long, dark eyelashes fan across her cheeks when she blinks, and just the slightest flush appears on her high cheekbones.

"Anything you would suggest?" I smile, and that beautiful light shade of pink grows deeper, making my heart swell.

The night goes well, and everyone at the table is stuffed. We've ordered extra over-the-top food and drinks. The waitress slides the ticket down, and I pick it up. When everyone but Harrison argues about wanting to pay, I put my hand up.

"Tonight is on me. Tomorrow, Harrison is buying,"

He narrows his eyes at me.

I know the fucker can more than cover the cost. He owns the most successful architectural firm in

Pennsylvania.

Everyone gets up and makes their way out of the restaurant. I pull Catherine to hang back.

"Don't touch me," she barks at me.

I throw my hands up.

"I only wanted to tell you we have a position opening at BU. It may not be something you want, but it can get your feet wet." It's a lie. I know she would want the position I'm about to propose.

She cocks an eyebrow, and I have to laugh a little on the inside at how easy this is.

"What position, and you better not say under you?"

If she only knew.

"It's for a fine arts teacher." I pause to get a read on her to see if she is biting. "As I said, it may not be what you want, but you can submit an application to me by the end of the week ... if you're interested." I start to walk off because I don't want to seem overly eager. I'm not ready to give more right now.

Her hand touches my arm to stop me, and I swear I can feel electricity going straight to my dick.

"Wait." She lets out a breath. "Yes, I'm very interested, and thank you for sharing."

We lock eyes, and I want so badly to kiss her, to run my fingers to the back of her neck and pull her flush with my body so she can feel the heat coursing through my veins.

CHAPTER SEVEN
Catherine

I stand like an idiot, staring at Mr. Largewood. I was being so ugly, thinking he was only after one thing. I shake my head, trying to find the right words.

"I'm sorry I was acting so rude. I just ... I'm not used to men being nice without wanting something in return. Thank you, and yes, I'm very interested. It's actually perfect. I love art. My major is education. Also, I give a free class at the Buckton Elementary School."

"Oh." Jackson's mouth drops. "I didn't know that."

I laugh. "How would you have known?" He seems genuinely surprised. He should know my degree or at least he could find out. He's the dean, for crying out loud. "But you do have access to our records. So, I guess I shouldn't have said that." I look away, feeling my cheeks heat up from those intense brown eyes.

Those deep chocolate eyes I could lose myself in.

His deep voice comes out in a baritone that sends

vibrations straight to my sex, and I feel the start of an orgasm.

How pathetic am I?

"You volunteer free art classes at Buckton Elementary?" Jackson asks, ignoring what I said about my degree.

"Yeah." We start walking to the parking lot where the rest of our group has gone. "I love it. My family was lower income, and my old art teacher gave me free classes. It gave me a way to express myself. That's the reason why I love art so much, and I want to give something back to honor her."

Jackson doesn't speak, and I think maybe I'm boring him. When we stop at the back of Claire's car, his hand comes to rest on my lower back.

"I had a very lovely dinner, Ms. Cane."

I nod and turn to get into the backseat of the Mini Cooper.

As soon as the doors close and Claire pulls out of the parking lot, Joey says, "What the fuck Catherine!" She never used my full name. I'm always Cat.

"Mr. Largewood is so fucking hot! Did you invite him back to the room, or did he invite you back to his? When are you going to hit that? I would so be on top of his cock riding him Cowgirl style." She stops only long enough to catch a breath before she starts again. She doesn't even give me time to speak.

"Well? Are you going to hit it? You better. You have a legal duty to fill, and that's to ride his cock and tell us all the details. I bet he's a freak in the sheets."

"You need to get laid, Catherine," Claire adds.

I roll my eyes.

Claire is the last person I would take advice from.

She's like a freaky horn ball. The girl is beautiful, and she knows it, but the one thing we don't have in common is that I'm not fucking anyone and haven't since my high school boyfriend.

"I'm so going to give it to Harrison. I'm meeting him to take a walk on the beach. Only I don't plan on walking; I only plan on riding his cock all the way up and down the beach." She says the last part a seductive purr.

"I have no doubt you will ride his cock," Susie chimes in.

We all laugh. That's the great thing about the friends I have. We get along so well and don't judge each other over what we choose to or shouldn't do.

They know I haven't been with anyone since Chris, and I really didn't have a desire until I saw Jackson. Even then, I knew he couldn't be mine. I'm just another student who was a fan of his good looks, and he's the dean of the university. Basically, he's way out of my league.

We're up in the condo and getting ready to watch a movie when there's a knock at the door.

Claire yells she'll it and runs out of the bathroom, opening the door to a waiting Harrison.

A small part of me is disappointed it wasn't Jackson.

She squeals, and we all turn to look when he hands her a rose.

Figures she would get excited over a simple rose. Doesn't he know he doesn't have to work so hard? She's already ready for him.

"Don't wait up!" she tells us with a wink and closes the door behind her.

Susie and Joey are stretched across the couch, sharing a blanket, and I've taken the oversized lounger.

Just as I get comfortable and press to play the movie, another knock occurs.

"Your turn," Susie and Joey yell out in unison.

I throw my blanket off and rise, yelling, "You should have packed…" Opening the door, I finish "Your key."

It's not Claire. It's Jackson in a sleeveless top and grey joggers that show his very large package. I swallow.

"Eyes up here, Ms. Cane." His smile is painfully breathtaking.

"Sorry, I just thought you were Claire coming back."

His smile never leaves his handsome features.

"I've never been mistaken for a woman before, but I don't think your friend will be back anytime soon. I have a feeling she won't be back tonight if I know Harrison."

Trying not to be affected by the large equipment showing in his joggers, I ask him, "Do you want to come in?"

He grins, and I can tell he was waiting for me to ask him.

"Yes, I wanted to see what you were doing. Since I will be alone, and it's only nine."

Joey and Susie both say hi, but they don't bother sitting up—each of their heads on the opposite of the couch.

Shit that means he'll have to sit with me.

CHAPTER EIGHT

Jackson

Catherine opens the door, and instantly, my eyes are drawn to her hard nipples. Her top is so thin, I can see her full and heavy tits through the sheer white material. I can't wait to have a mouthful of them while she's riding my cock.

Fuck me! I'm going to be stroking my cock at the sight of those perfect tits.

When I finally get invited to come inside, she leads me in, and I get a perfect view of that plump ass in those short shorts. I have to adjust my erection, and will it to come down.

Joey and her other friend, who I can't seem to remember her name, both say hello, and I notice the only seat left is the oversized lounger in a corner to the side of the couch. It's facing the open patio doors looking out to the ocean—the sounds of which echo through the small condo.

"Well, as you can see, there's not much furniture in

here, but you're welcome to sit with me," she climbs into her seat, and I follow her.

Her vanilla scent invades my nostrils again, and my boner is poking me in the lower abdomen.

Fuck me! I hope I get through this night.

It's been two weeks since I've talked to Catherine.

After the night when we shared a chair for all of five minutes before my Candy Cane made her excuses and scurried off, we haven't spoken or seen each other. I was starting to think she didn't want the position.

I smile, looking down at her application for the teaching position. Catherine turned in her paperwork last week, and I've been holding off on telling her she has the job. I don't want her to think anything about how fast the decision was made.

I pull my cell from my pocket, dial her number, and when she answers in that voice I hear in my wet dreams, I almost groan.

"Hello," she says again.

"Catherine," I breathe into the phone.

"Yes. Is this Mr. Largewood?"

"Jackson, please."

"Jackson," her voice is soft.

"Catherine, I was calling to let you know you have the position if you want it." There's silence on the other end. "Catherine, are you there?"

"Yes, I'm here."

I can hear music in the background.

I wonder if she is at home or work.

I don't remember her having to work tonight. When I hear a male voice, I jump up from my chair.

"Catherine, where are you?" I'm fuming with rage.

"I'm at..." The phone goes quiet. "Hold on a minute," she yells. "Let me step outside."

I hear a male voice telling her not to be gone too long. I grab my keys off my desk, take two large strides, and slam my office door shut. I'm fucking pissed because no one is to touch her. She's mine and no one else's.

She finally comes back to the phone, "Sorry about that. I'm hanging out with my brother. He moved into a new apartment." She's silent for a brief moment. "Jackson, are you still there?"

It's her brother. Thank fuck!

"Yeah ... I'm headed out for the evening. I was closing up my office. Are you still interested in the position? It's yours." I wait for her to respond, and when she does, I just about jump with excitement.

"Yes, very interested."

"Okay, just come by my office on Monday and fill out the papers. Mrs. Thomas has to leave after Thanksgiving, and we really need you to finish the semester for her. She can fill you in with all the details. I know you won't get your degree 'til the end of the semester, but we're all aware of it, and it's no problem."

We hang up after she mentions that she'll be at my office Monday morning.

My weekend just got better!

It's Saturday night, and I'm ready to let loose and

enjoy a few drinks with the guys.

I sit in my usual booth, waiting for them to get here. Harrison slides into the booth, grinning.

I throw an eyebrow up. "What?"

"I'm just wondering if you've gotten your dick sucked lately?"

"You know I don't make a show of when or who sucks my cock." I pick up my scotch and take a sip.

"Yep, well, here's to me then." Harrison holds his drink up in the air.

I hold up my drink, and he clinks his against it.

"I'm guessing you haven't hit it yet?" Harrison states.

I raise an eyebrow.

"Jackson, all jokes aside. Just ask her out on a date. Everyone can see how you look at her. You're like a fucking lost puppy. I've never seen you look so lost in someone. I know I give you shit, but come on, man, you've waited long enough. She'll be graduating soon, and you won't have to worry about dating a student."

"I wish it was that simple." I look at him and debate if I should tell him. Fuck it. He's one of my best friends. "I hired her."

"You fucking what!"

"Keep your voice down." I look over to see if Catherine has taken the stage yet. "I said I hired her."

"What the fuck did you do that for?" he asks in a lower tone than before.

I shrug my shoulders. "I was thinking I don't want her leaving. I want to keep her close, and I think fucking her while we roll around in paint from her art room would be some sexy shit!" I grin.

Flashes of Catherine naked with wet paint covering

her tits, ass, and stomach while I drive into her warm wet pussy, while she slides around on the floor screaming my name, is something that would be worth every moment I've waited.

Harrison just laughs as though he thinks that's all I'm after, and I let him think it. He just doesn't know I'm fucking her for keeps. I plan on my dick being the best she's ever had ... and the last.

CHAPTER NINE

Catherine

Today was my first day teaching art classes as a professor.

Professor Cane. It has a nice ring to it.

"Well done, Professor Cane," a deep voice booms behind me.

Class is over, and the students have left. I'm straightening up after my last class for the day.

"Thank you, Dean Largewood." His eyes are blazing, and I can tell he's up to no good. I used to want those eyes to look at me. Now that I'm working as a professor, I don't think sleeping with or having lustful thoughts about my boss is the best idea. "How long have you been watching?"

I already know he came in within the last twenty minutes. I felt his presence the moment he walked in. He has this alpha dominance aura about him that radiates big dick energy. You can feel his energy just being in the same room. It rolls off of him in waves.

His grin deepens to a large smile. "Hmm, I think we both know how long I've been watching you." His eyes sweep over me, and I can feel the heat from them as my face turns hot.

"Have dinner with me tonight," he states.

Hmm. "Business or pleasure?" I ask, trying to hide my face by not breaking my rhythm cleaning the brushes.

"Pleasure. There will be so much pleasure for you. You'll want a second entrée of my very special dish—my cock," he says with seduction.

I swallow the craving of wanting him.

It can only live in my thoughts. I need this job. I have to get experience if I ever decide to leave and go somewhere else. Having him will only ever be a fantasy.

He raises an eyebrow when I take a moment too long to reply.

Finally, I look up and answer.

"No, I don't think that would be wise. We need to keep things on a professional level."

Slowly, he shakes his head. His eyes darken, and I feel his anger stab at me. I can see the calculating look in his eyes, knowing it's something I won't like.

"Is that a hard no, Professor Cane?"

I swallow back my fear so it won't take over to give in.

"Yes." It's barely audible, but I said it.

He rises from the desk in the back of the room.

"I believe I can change your mind," he says with too much self-assurance.

Our eyes stay locked as he crosses the room. "You see, Professor Cane. I think you need this job, and I'm more than happy to help. It's hard to come by a job in your field, especially something of this caliber." He circles around me. "I happen to know that you work at the largest strip and sex club in the state."

I close my eyes. There it is. His Ace.

"I also know that you would hate it to get out to the students who would catcall you and laugh at you in your class rather than take you seriously and pay attention to your teaching." He takes his time circling me. "Wouldn't you hate that, Professor Cane?"

My eyes are still closed when he whispers his last sentence in my ear.

"You need this job, and I need to bury my cock so deep inside of you that you'll feel me for days." His lips place soft kisses on my neck as I stand frozen.

He slips a piece of paper in my hand. "Be there tonight." Then he walks out of my classroom.

I grab my briefcase with force and follow behind him, words I didn't even know I knew leaving my lips.

I look at myself in the rearview mirror. "Why are you here," I ask quietly. I should throw in my paint brushes, but teaching has always been a dream of mine. I love painting. It helps relax me in a way nothing ever has.

We were poor, and when my teacher offered to teach me free classes, my parents jumped at the suggestion. I knew it was because they didn't want me around, and I didn't want to be around to have to deal with their fighting.

They fought over money and how to get enough to pay the bills. Escaping to another world always helped during their heated arguments. It smoothed the storm I felt inside because of their disagreements.

I get out of my car and walk toward the restaurant. My nerves are standing on the edge of a cliff, ready to jump.

Jackson's note only stated an address where to meet him. I was surprised when I searched the address and found it was Amber's. I was expecting him to give me his home address. After all, he is blackmailing me. Blackmailing me to sleep with him. So why would he want to go out to dinner first? Especially somewhere like this. Amber's just happens to be the most expensive restaurant in the city.

When I walk under the sign lit up reading Amber's, I'm met with an elevator. It's on the twelfth floor of a stunning all-glass building, and I have heard nothing but how delicious the food is.

After I enter the elevator, my mind goes wild with why, of all people, he would want to be with me. He's one of the sexiest men in the city. He comes from money and has money in his own right. He was named in the top ten men of the city's most eligible bachelors. So, why would he want to blackmail me? He could get sex from anyone.

The elevator stops, and when the doors open, I'm immediately starstruck. Jackson is standing against the wall on his phone. He's already tall at six feet, but his black suit makes him look even taller, if possible. His red tie complements his suit, which fits his sculpted body, displaying all the defined muscles in his arms and broad shoulders. Butterflies flutter in my belly, making their way to my throat and causing my mouth to dry.

He peers up at me and gives me that perfect smile. On autopilot, my core heats up, replacing the butterflies. The fire in my core grows, wanting him to use my body in whatever way he wants.

I'm so fucked! Literally.

CHAPTER TEN

Jackson

Sitting across from Catherine, I think about how I'm going to have this night go. Should I let her warmup to the idea of me being buried deep inside her, or should I take her into the ladies' room and bend her over the sink? The night will go however I want, after all. I always get what I want when I want it.

"Jackson, did you hear me?"

I want to say, 'No." I want to say, 'I'm too busy picturing you being tied up and gagged while I fuck you,' but I don't. Instead, I reply, "No, I was too busy admiring your dress. I'm glad you wore it. The red sets off your hair."

When Catherine blushes, it gives her cheeks the perfect shade of rose.

"Thank you for the dress. You didn't have to send it. I have clothes to wear. I don't think what you are after is a courtship." Whispering, Catherine says, "I think we both know what you want."

I smirk. I know she can see my thoughts being played out across my face.

"Well," I lean closer to her. "Tell me what it is that you think I want."

She rolls her eyes.

"You want sex," she says quickly. "You're blackmailing me into having sex with you."

I let out a laugh filled with sexual promises.

"What I want is not just sex, Professor Cane. I want your body to submit to me." My eyes travel to her breasts. "I want you to scream for the gods above when I'm pounding into that beautiful, delicious tight pussy."

Her jaw falls open.

Oh my my. I am going to have so much fun training her.

My smile grows as I watch her heavy breasts rise and fall with her breathing.

She's completely turned on.

Just the thought of her wet heat has me hard as a rock, and I can't wait any longer to have her. Fuck waiting. I need to be inside her.

I pull out my wallet and toss a few hundred on the table. Folding it back into my pocket, I extend my hand to Catherine.

"Let's go. I want to get some dessert. I know a place not too far from here."

She places her small hand in mine, and we walk to the elevator. I plan on leading her to my car, but she stops me when we reach the front door.

"I have my car. I can follow you."

I know if I let her go, she won't follow me. I'm not going to let that happen. I hold tightly to her hand.

"We can come back and get your car."

Leading her to my car, I unlock the doors and open the passenger side. I watch as she sits in the seat. The red dress I purchased for her slides up her thighs, and I don't see panties.

I shut the door and walk to the driver's side, squeezing my cock for a little relief before I reach my door.

I need to fuck her before I go insane.

I get behind the wheel, crank the accelerator, and drive over the speed limit to get to my house. I live in a fucking Mr. Rogers neighborhood, but I love the quietness it offers. I bought the large colonial to have a quieter, slower pace of living, and it's the perfect place for Catherine to scream without being heard.

We're leaving the city when Catherine asks, "Where are we going?"

"Trust me."

Catherine remains quiet, and twenty minutes later, I pull into the long driveway that leads to my house. Clicking the remote control on my sun visor, the single garage door opens, and I pull in, shutting it once we are parked.

I tilt my head to the door that leads inside. "Come on, I've got some tasty treats inside." I get out of the car and see that Catherine is still sitting inside.

She's looking through the front windshield with an expression of shock. So, I walk over to her door, open it, and grab her hand.

"Come on, my Candy Cane, I won't bite. However, I do want to see how many licks I can make before you come."

I don't miss how she subtly clenches her thighs together.

Fuck, I can't wait.

Pulling her out of her seat, we walk through the kitchen, and I whirl her around, pinning her against the island.

"Tell me, Candy," I put my hand on her thighs and push her dress up. "Are you wearing any panties?" My voice is thick with lust when I slide my hand over the soft, bare skin. "No panties. You naughty girl."

I can feel her body tremble.

"Jackson, I don't think we should be—"

I cut her off when I take her lips in a brutal kiss. She doesn't resist me, opening her mouth and welcoming my tongue. Swirling our tongues together, I reach around to grab a hand full of her ass and growl into her mouth. Fuck, it's so firm. When I reach back with my other hand, I grab the second ass cheek and squeeze both hard. Lifting her onto the island, I break our kiss, then taking a step back, I push her legs apart. When I see her glistening shaved pussy, I grab my cock through my pants and give it a little tug.

"Oh, Candy, that's the prettiest pussy I've ever seen. I need a taste. Spread your legs wider."

Her face reddens, but she's a good girl and spreads them wide for me. Our eyes are locked, and I can tell her pupils are dilated. My hand and her eyes haven't left my cock.

"Do you want my cock? Do you want to be a good girl and suck me off?"

She nods. When she speaks, her voice comes out raspy, "I want to be your good girl."

Her pussy drips onto the kitchen island.

"Oh baby, I want you to be my girl, but first, I need to taste this sweet pussy."

I spread my hand on her chest and gently push her back. She leans on her elbows, watching me lean in between her legs. I stick out my tongue and run it up her pussy, from that tight hole I'm dying to fuck to her clit.

"Oh, baby girl," I breathe against her pussy. "Mmm, you taste like my favorite vanilla milkshake."

I lick her again, then reach for what I already put out on the counter, hoping this would be happening tonight. I grab a candy cane and open it.

"What are you going to do with that?"

Grinning I break off a piece putting it in my mouth. When I dip my face down, I run my tongue along her clit and roll the candy cane along with it.

Catherine moans and drops her head back.

I suck her clit, and her legs wrap around my head.

"Do you like my tongue on your pussy?"

She moans loudly, so I go back to my treat, sucking and licking, rolling the candy cane over her clit one more time. Her orgasm hits her, and I lap it up, enjoying her sweetness.

When I pull away, I swipe my hand over my mouth.

"Come here," I pull her off the counter and spin her around. Setting my hands on her shoulders, I push her down to her knees, "Pull me out."

I watch her small fingers undo my slacks. When she gets them open, I hiss when she tries to wrap her hand around my cock.

"Suck me. I want to hear you gagging while sucking my cock."

She sticks out her tongue, and when I think she's about to run it along the head of my cock, she surprises me as her face moves lower, and she licks my balls.

"Fuck me," I hiss out, falling back against the kitchen island.

Her mouth replaces her tongue, sucking my balls as her hand strokes my shaft. I'm about two seconds away from coming and haven't even been inside her.

"Fuck Candy, get up. I need to be inside your pussy. Are you on the pill?"

"Yes, but we should use protection."

"I'm clean, are you?"

She nods.

That's all I need before I lift her up and slam her down on my cock. She screams, her nails digging into my shoulders.

My eyes go wide. "Are you a virgin?"

Tears run down her face. "No." Her voice is strained. "It's just … it's been a long time."

"How long?"

She swallows and rests her head on my shoulder.

"Tell me," I say quietly.

"Since my high school boyfriend was killed in a car accident."

I feel her tears stain my dress shirt.

"Look at me." She lifts her head, and immediately, my head tells me blackmailing her wasn't right. I want to be selfish and really start thrusting my cock into her, but instead, I bend to let her crawl off me, but she doesn't.

"Don't do that. I don't want you feeling sorry for me." She places a soft kiss on my lips.

"Fuck me," she whispers.

CHAPTER ELEVEN

Catherine

Jackson's lips swallow the hurt my heart feels. I close my eyes and get lost in his taste and his touch. He trails kisses from my chin down to my neck, nipping gently as he goes.

I feel arousal coursing through my veins, and I start riding his cock. It doesn't take but two lifts, and on the next lift he slams me down, forcing me to take every painfully thick inch. I shouldn't love it, but the burn of being stretched by him only turns me on more. Closing my mouth, I grit my teeth through the pain of being stretched from his girth.

I didn't know a man's dick could be so big.

His lips brush against my ear, and his breathing is heavy.

"Catherine, you're so tight and wet. You feel so fucking good wrapped around my cock."

I kiss and suck his neck, biting down as his hips move at a piston pace.

"Don't hold back. I want to hear those screams as you come on my cock while I fill you up with every drop of my cum."

He slides one arm under my leg, then mirrors it on the other side until my legs rest on his biceps. He brutally thrusts into me, and my head falls back from the feeling of him being buried so deep in me. He's reaching places I never knew existed.

"That's it. Let me hear you scream my name while you're coming all over my cock."

Thrust after thrust, my clit gets assaulted until I cry out, "I'm coming."

My back hits the counter, and he thrusts into me twice more before he grunts his release and pushes his hips forward one last time. I feel his cock jerk and his cum coats my inner walls.

"Fuck," he says as he places kisses along my neck. "You're not going home tonight. I want you in my bed."

The next evening, Jackson drives me to my car. When he pulls up, I start to get out, but Jackson's his hand comes to halt me.

"What are your plans for tonight?"

"I have to work, but somehow, I think you know that."

His eyes darken. "The only job you should have besides teaching is riding my cock."

I roll my eyes. "You may be blackmailing me for sex, but you won't be telling me what to do. After all, why should I give you something when you keep blackmailing me?"

I jerk my door open and close it behind me. When I get into my car, I lock it so he can't make any more demands. One night is all we've spent together, and he thinks he owns me.

Jackson knocks on the window and points his finger in a motion for me to roll down the window.

"What?" I huff out.

"Catherine, I'm not playing. You will quit that job."

"Jackson, I'm a grown woman." I glare daggers at him. "I don't need you to tell me what to do." I put my car in reverse, then drive off.

Fuck him!

I go home, grab a shower, and start getting dressed to head to work when my phone pings.

Jackson: *I mean it, Catherine. I don't want to hear of you showing your tits to anyone.*

I don't reply.

Who does he think he is? I slam my blush brush down on the counter. Walking into the bedroom, I gather my outfit for tonight, and stuff it into my bag.

I head out and drive to the club. As I walk to the dressing room, the owner is coming out and stops at the door.

"Catherine," his eyes widen.

"Mitchell."

"Catherine, we don't need you tonight. We have enough girls to work. So, you can head home if you like."

"I really need the money." Which isn't a lie. I do

need the money. I want to pay off all my school loans early. I've been working hard to keep low balances, but with going to the beach and Joey's wedding coming up, I could use the extra cash.

Mitchell looks pale. I frown, worried he may be sick.

"Are you okay? You look pale."

"Fine, I'm fine." He quickly moves past me.

That's strange.

I open the door and notice that Jane is the only person in the dressing room. She's sliding up her thong.

That answers that. I guess Jane and Mitchell must have been doing a little tickle-and-play.

CHAPTER TWELVE

Jackson

Mitchell comes out from the dark hallway that leads to the women's dressing room. He sees me sitting in our usual spot and makes his way over to slide into the booth.

"You ready for this?"

I tilt my head, wondering what he could be asking, but then I realize he's talking about Catherine.

"She's here?" My hands curl into fists.

"Yeah, but you need to keep your shit together. This is my business, and I don't want any fucking drama. Got it?"

I grit my teeth. "Got it."

I hear whistles. Turning my sight in the direction of the stage, Catherine is walking out in candy cane stockings, a red bra, and shorts that are short enough to show her beautiful plump ass. My dick doesn't even twitch. It goes from limp to hard as a fucking hammer in seconds, waiting to nail Catherine.

"Fuck!" Mitchell's mouth drops open.

Glancing over to him, I see his eyes are wide, and they roam over Catherine's figure. Jealousy kicks in, especially when I hear all the other men whistling and making provocative comments.

I can't sit and watch this any longer. I rise to my feet, determined not to allow this to happen to the only woman I've ever had more feelings for other than just wanting to fuck.

Catherine spins around on the stage, taking off her bra, leaving only pasties to cover her pink nipples. The same nipples I had in my mouth last night.

My fucking nipples.

Her eyes rest on me when she comes to a stop from her spin around the pole. I can see fear in them.

I told her I wouldn't allow her to come back, and I meant it. I knew she would be back, and that's why I came tonight. She's all I want. I didn't need to come here, but I was determined if she showed up to haul her ass out of here.

I stalk to her with a cold expression on my face.

Her eyes never leave mine as I walk up to the stage and hop onto it. When I bend down, we stand nose to nose.

My chest heaves with anger.

"Don't–"

She doesn't complete her sentence. I throw her over my shoulder and leap off the stage, heading to the dressing room.

Catherine pounds on my back and kicks her feet while the men complain about me snatching her off the stage.

Fuck them!

I step into the dressing room, slam the door closed, and throw Catherine on the small sofa. Her perfect tits bounce. Making quick work to unzip my pants, I pull my cock out, giving it a tug.

"Jackson," she tries to get up. "You can't pull me off the stage like that. You don't own me."

I wrap my hand around her neck, forcing her into submission. A smirk pulls at my lips as she lies down on her back.

I can feel her pulse beating fast.

Catherine snakes her hand under my balls, squeezing them. If she thinks that hurts, she's wrong.

"Fuck, baby." My breathing is heavy. "Pull off the string that covers my pretty pink pussy. I'm going to fill you up with my cock."

Her eyes turn to slits. "What if I don't?"

I reach down and rip them off. Catherine gasps.

"I can smell you." I say, arching my eyebrow. "Feel your heart racing. You want my cock. Now spread those legs, and let me see what's mine."

Her hand moves from my balls to my cock, tugging it as she slowly spreads her legs for me. I push myself into her hand, and she pumps me.

"Oh, baby, I have thought of nothing else but this cunt."

I take her hand away from my cock and pull her by the legs down the couch. Climbing between them, I angle my throbbing cock at her entrance and ease into her wetness. We both moan at the sensitive sensations of our bodies connecting.

"You like my cock, baby?" Slowly pulling out, I stop, waiting for a response. "Eyes right here, baby. I want you to look at me." She opens her bright blue orbs. They're so vibrant, I could get lost in them.

I push into her hard, making sure I'm balls deep into her. She yelps.

"Tell me how much you like my cock." I pull back out.

Wetting her lips, she whispers, "Yes."

I thrust into her again, harder this time.

"Tell me how much."

I pull out of her drawing back, grab her hips, and flip her over. "Get on your hands and knees," I growl when her round ass is stuck up in the air, displaying her back entrance. Swiping my fingers through her wet folds, I move my fingers up to rub her clit.

Catherine moans loudly.

"You like that, baby?"

"Oh God, yes!" Her voice is filled with heated desire.

Her words send me spiraling into a hunger to feel her coming on my cock. I hold on to her hips, digging my fingers into her soft flesh, and take her with a need to show her my ownership over her body. It belongs to me now. It's not for her to show to anyone else. Her screams are muffled as her face gets buried in the cushion with each thrust into her sweetness.

When we both find our release, I collapse on top of her, pushing her body down on the couch. I'm not ready to pull out of her yet … or ever. I never want to leave the sweetest, heavenly pussy I've ever stuck my cock in.

CHAPTER THIRTEEN
Catherine

It's been six weeks since Jackson pulled me off the stage at Vipers. After having sex in the dressing room, he packed up my vanity desk and wouldn't listen to me when I refused to quit.

After fucking me the second time up against the door, he talked me into leaving.

It's a damn shame how he uses his magic dick to get anything he wants. A man shouldn't be so blessed with a cock that good.

I close my classroom door behind me, heading down the hallway to Jackson's office. I shoved some candy canes in my purse since they have become his ultimate favorite candy. Thank goodness it's close to Christmas so that I can keep an endless supply.

When I turn the corner, I hear laughing coming from Jackson's office. His deep laughter sends a volt of electricity straight to my core.

Why does everything about him have to be so sexual?

When I hear my name mentioned, I stop. Doing my best, I listen to what he's saying.

"I'm glad you finally fucked her. I swear all we heard about was how you were going to nail her to the wall." a male voice says.

My eyebrows furrow. *I know that voice. Mitchell.*

Jackson laughs. "Nailed her to your dressing room door."

"Fuck man, I couldn't tell you how many women have hung on that door begging for God to help them."

They both laugh.

Am I just a fuck for him? Someone to conquer?

"You ready to head out for lunch?" I hear Jackson gathering his keys. "I want to get back to see Catherine before she leaves for the day," Jackson remarks.

"Oh, that's right. You're going to make that fantasy of sliding around in wet paint a reality." I hear Mitchell rise up from the chair.

I stand my ground. I want Jackson to see me. I want him to know I used him for this job just as much as he used me for my body, just like my high school boyfriend.

Travis Gunn was my high school boyfriend. He was killed in a motorcycle accident. At the funeral, I found out he slept with half of the cheerleaders at our school. It took me by surprise when my so-called friend threw it in my face that he only slept with me to take my virginity.

Jackson and Mitchell come out of the office, and Jackson's face turns red.

Good. Fucker!

"Catherine, we were about to go out for lunch."

I give him a forced smile. Turning to Mitchell, I say, "Stacey called and said she couldn't make it in tonight, so I told her I would work her shift." I'm not really working at Vipers, but I feel like fucking with Jackson.

I turn my attention back to Jackson. "You guys have a good lunch." I pull out my candy cane and pop it in my mouth. "I'm off to get a hammer."

I turn on my heels, and walk back down the hallway.

"Catherine!" Jackson yells, I hear his heavy footsteps coming up behind me. "Catherine." Jackson's hand wraps around my arm, twirling me around, "Catherine, I told you that you're not working there anymore."

"You don't tell me what to do." My finger comes up to his chest, poking him. "You got what you wanted. You nailed me to the wall, or was it the door?" I raise my eyebrows.

"It's not like that."

"No, really? Tell me. What was it like, Jackson? You wanted to sleep with me, and now what? You're going to do what Mitchell does, sleep with other women? That's what men do when they get what they want. They want to sleep with anyone that gives it to them."

"It's not like that." He pulls me closer, "You overheard us. Didn't you?"

I look down at my shaking hands. "Yes." Looking back up to make eye contact with him, I straighten my spine. "Was I just a conquest for you?" My voice is soft and weak. I hate being vulnerable.

"At first,"—he shakes his head—"but not now…

Now, I want to keep you. I'm not ready to ask for marriage, but I'm so serious about you that..." He swallows. "I want you to move in with me."

Shocked, tears brim the edge of my eyes.

"Are you just asking because I caught you talking shit?"

"Not at all." His hands come up to caress my face. "I'm asking because I want to wake up to you every morning."

"I don't think you mean that."

"Baby, I couldn't be more serious. I want to wake up with you beside me every morning, and waking up to your pussy wouldn't hurt, either."

I laugh, and a tear escapes my eye.

"Promise me if you ever think you want someone else, you'll tell me and not cheat on me."

He shakes his head. "I'm not going to cheat."

"Promise me," I demand.

"Look at me." His hands wipe the tears from my eyes. "I'm too old for that bullshit. You're the one for me. I've never met anyone who can hold my interest. You make me wake up with a smile and a hard cock every morning. Your pussy is gold. I want to lock it up in an iron-clad safe." He brings his forehead to rest on mine, "Tell me you'll move in with me."

I close my eyes and nod, rubbing our foreheads together.

"I've got more candy canes in my purse," I whisper so Mitchell can't hear me.

"Mitchell, I'll catch you later. I'm eating at my favorite buffet." Jackson pulls me back to his office, walking past a defeated Mitchell, shaking his head.

"Puss—" Mitchell calls out.

Jackson slams the door in his face, cutting him off.

"Baby, get on my desk, spread those pretty thighs, and lay out that buffet for me. I can't wait to devour what's mine."

Make sure to follow Aurelia on Amazon to keep in the know of new releases.

ABOUT THE AUTHOR

Aurelia writes dark and contemporary romance and enjoys reading it just as much! She lives in Alabama with her husband, daughter, and fur babies. She spends most of her time caring for her loved ones and plotting stories. She's excited to share her stories and to grow as an author. Look for more outstanding stories from Aurelia by following her on social media.

Made in the USA
Columbia, SC
27 April 2025